PUFFIN

Julius Caesar's Goat

Dick King-Smith served in the Grenadier Guards during the Second World War, and afterwards spent twenty years as a farmer in Gloucestershire, the county of his birth. Many of his stories are inspired by his farming experiences. Later he taught at a village primary school. His first book, *The Fox Busters*, was published in 1978. Since then he has written a great number of children's books, including *The Sheep-Pig* (winner of the Guardian Award and filmed as *Babe*), *Harry's Mad*, *Noah's Brother*, *The Hodgeheg*, *Martin's Mice*, *Ace*, *The Cuckoo Child* and *Harriet's Hare* (winner of the Children's Book Award in 1995). At the British Book Awards in 1991 he was voted Children's Author of the Year. He has three children, a large number of grandchildren and several great-grandchildren, and lives in a seventeenth-century cottage only a crow's flight from the house where he was born.

Dick King-Smith
Julius Caesar's Goat

Illustrated by Harry Horse

PUFFIN

PUFFIN BOOKS

Published by the Penguin Group
Penguin Books Ltd, 80 Strand, London WC2R 0RL, England
Penguin Group (USA), Inc., 375 Hudson Street, New York, New York 10014, USA
Penguin Books Australia Ltd, 250 Camberwell Road, Camberwell, Victoria 3124, Australia
Penguin Books Canada Ltd, 10 Alcorn Avenue, Toronto, Ontario, Canada M4V 3B2
Penguin Books India (P) Ltd, 11 Community Centre, Panchsheel Park, New Delhi – 110 017, India
Penguin Books (NZ) Ltd, Cnr Rosedale and Airborne Roads, Albany, Auckland, New Zealand
Penguin Books (South Africa) (Pty) Ltd, 24 Sturdee Avenue, Rosebank 2196, South Africa

Penguin Books Ltd, Registered Offices: 80 Strand, London WC2R 0RL, England

www.penguin.com

This story first appeared in *Just in Time* published by Penguin Books 1999
Text copyright © Fox Busters Ltd, 1999
This version first published 2000
4

Text copyright © Fox Busters Ltd, 2000
Illustrations copyright © Harry Horse, 2000
All rights reserved

The moral right of the author and illustrator has been asserted

Set in Baskerville MT

Made and printed in England by Clays Ltd, St Ives plc

British Library Cataloguing in Publication Data
A CIP catalogue record for this book is available from the British Library

ISBN 0–141–30682–3

Chapter One

You might think you know quite a bit about Julius Caesar. I bet you didn't know that he had absolutely no sense of smell.

Though his parents were not all that bright – his father's name was Crassus Idioticus and his mother was called Stupida – Julius was in fact a quick-witted boy, with excellent hearing and twenty-twenty vision. But from the age of ten onwards he couldn't smell a thing. He couldn't smell bread baking or meat roasting, and the scent of flowers meant nothing to him.

It happened like this.

Julius, who had been born in the year 100 BC, was playing with a lot of other boys in the playground at North Rome Primary School. It was 15 March (the Ides of March, the Romans called it) 90 BC and they were playing with a large round ball made of a cow's stomach packed with scraps of rags from old togas.

The game was called Foot-the-Ball, and the idea was to kick it

between two posts. The only person
allowed to touch the ball with his
hands was called the Keeper of the
Goal, and that is what Caesar was
that particular morning.

There was a great flurry in the
mouth of the goal and one of
Julius's opponents, a rough boy
called Brutus, took a spectacular
overhead kick at the ball and missed

it. His foot hit Julius smack on the nose.

'*Et tu, Brute!*' cried Julius (which, loosely translated, means 'It would be you, you brute!') and he retired, hurt.

Stupida was horrified when her son arrived home with his handsome Roman nose all swollen. So swollen, in fact, that even Crassus Idioticus noticed.

But the swelling went down and Julius's nose looked much as it had before, apart from a slight bend in the middle. But it didn't work any more. Julius Caesar had lost his sense of smell for ever.

They took him to all the best medical men in Rome, sparing no

4

expense, but none could help. However, the oldest and wisest one said to Julius, 'You must count your blessings, young man. The world may be full of pleasant smells, but it is also filled with horrible stinks and stenches, which now will never worry you.'

Julius Caesar never forgot this wise old man's remark, and many years later, when he was already a famous soldier, he used his handicap to great advantage.

In 49 BC, he was commanding an army in Gaul and decided to attack another army led by a man called Pompey. To do this, he had to cross a stream called the Rubicon.

On the banks of this stream was a

herd of goats, which Caesar's
legionaries, always eager for fresh
meat, quickly killed to eat for lunch.
Amongst the nanny goats was one
very large billy goat with long ginger
hair and a pair of sweeping horns.
He broke free from the soldiers and
ran, bleating loudly, towards Julius

Caesar himself as he strode down to the water's edge, surrounded by his bodyguard.

Hastily the bodyguard drew back because of the appalling smell that the billy goat gave out. All billy goats stink, but this one was a champion stinker.

Then a brave centurion stepped forward. 'O Caesar!' he cried. 'Wilt thou have this beast for lunch?' He waited, sword upraised, his eyes on his leader's right hand.

If Caesar's thumb had then been turned down, one swipe would have removed the animal's head from its body.

Caesar looked down at the billy goat. He was impressed by the look in its eyes, a look much more intelligent than that of Crassus Idioticus or Stupida.

Meanwhile, the watching soldiers marvelled. There was Caesar, standing right by the stinking creature, even laying his hand upon its head!

'O great Caesar!' they whispered to each other. 'What courage!'

Little did they know that he couldn't smell a thing.

Still the brave centurion waited, his sword upraised, holding his nose with the other hand.

Then Caesar said, '*Hircus audens est*' (which, loosely translated, means, 'That goat's got bottle'), and he put his thumb up.

The centurion lowered his sword, and Julius Caesar, closely followed by his goat, waded into the water and crossed the Rubicon.

Chapter Two

Now, as his legions prepared to march south to confront the army of Pompey, Caesar issued an order with regard to his new pet. Caesar's goat was to be given all possible honour, and anyone found guilty of treating it with disrespect would be put to death.

As for the man who would have executed the animal if the general's thumb had turned down, he, much to his dismay, was appointed Centurion-Capricorn. Not even a rise in pay of one *denarius per diem* (a penny a day) could compensate him for having now to live permanently

next to that awful pong, but of course he could not complain.

'*Caseus durus!*' his mates whispered to him (which, loosely translated, means 'Hard cheese!').

Now, as the legions moved south, Julius Caesar and his bodyguard, along with the Centurion-Capricorn and the animal itself, marched in the middle of the column of soldiers.

At first the wind was in the south and thus blew in their faces.

It was a strong wind, so all those marching in front of Caesar were in luck, for they were spared the smell of the billy goat. All those behind Caesar, however, caught the full impact of the wind-borne stink.

They struggled along, holding

their noses and trying not to breathe
in. Luckily for them, however, the
wind soon changed. Now it was
blowing steadily from the north and

14

it was the turn of the soldiers
marching in front of Caesar to
cough and splutter at the awful
smell. It blew from the north all the
rest of the day, by which time the
soldiers at the front were absolutely

15

fed up. But no one dared say a word to Caesar.

Then someone among these forward troops had a brilliant idea.

'If only that goat marched in front of us,' he said, 'right at the head of the column, the wind would carry the smell away from us too.'

Then someone else had an even more brilliant idea.

'What if Pompey's army were ahead of us? If we were free of the stink and they were being suffocated by it? Why, before they'd recovered from the shock, we could make mincemeat of them!'

'By Jupiter! They'd all be gasping and choking, like we are now, and their eyes would be running, like ours are now, and they wouldn't be able to fight for toffee!'

'Yes, but how can we persuade Caesar to put the brute at the head of the army? "Why?" he'd say, and we couldn't say, "Because it stinks so bad." That'd be disrespect and we'd be topped.'

'What can we do then?'

'I know!' said a smarmy little legionary called Oleaginus. 'Leave it to me. I'll fix it.'

That night when they set up camp, Oleaginus made his way to Julius Caesar's tent to crave an audience with the general.

He found Caesar feeding his goat, while behind him stood the Centurion-Capricorn, holding a fold

of his toga discreetly over his nose.

'What is it, soldier?' said the
general.

'O great Caesar!' said Oleaginus
in his oiliest voice. 'I come with a

request from all my fellow
legionaries.'

'A request? What about?'

'About that most beautiful of
creatures, Your Excellency's goat.'

'What about it?'

'O great Caesar!' said Oleaginus. 'If only this noble animal could lead us into battle! How the sight of it, at the head of the army, would inspire every man behind it, while at the same time striking terror into the hearts of Your Excellency's foes!'

'D'you really think so?' said Caesar.

'Truly, O great Caesar!' replied Oleaginus in a choking voice, with his eyes streaming. The stench of the billy goat in the confined space of the tent was overpowering.

Ye Gods! thought Caesar, observing the legionary's tears. The poor fellow's overcome with emotion. Already my men have come to think of my goat as a mascot. With him to lead them, they'll fight like lions!

So it was that when Caesar's army struck camp next morning to continue the southward march, with the north wind still at their backs, the two leading figures in the long column of soldiers were the Centurion-Capricorn and the goat.

When at long last the two opposing armies met, they would have seemed to an observer to be equally matched. On either side were three legions, each of 3,000 men. Within each legion were 10 cohorts, each of 300 men. Within each cohort were 3 centuries, each of 100 men.

But it was an ill wind that blew in the faces of Pompey's army that day, for it carried upon it a thick, choking, acrid smell. When it reached them, Pompey's leading troops began first to falter and then to turn away in panic, rank after rank pushing and shoving back through their fellows in an effort to escape that ghastly stench until at last the whole army turned tail in a wild stampede.

The history books may tell you that Caesar defeated Pompey in the civil war between those two generals.

Rubbish!

Pompey and his legions were routed by Julius Caesar's goat.

Chapter Three

With the goat at the head of his
army, Caesar was unbeatable.
Sometimes he wondered why it was
that his goat seemed to be so
powerful a weapon, and occasionally
he asked his senior officers for their
opinion on the matter.

They of course, fearing for their

lives, could not mention the dreadful
smell. They still didn't know that
Caesar was quite unaware of it. So
they all agreed to say that they
thought the goat must have magical
properties, against which no foe
could stand.

Sometimes in their enthusiasm
they would overdo their praise of the
animal. And then Julius Caesar had
to remind them that, though his goat
(and its Centurion-Capricorn) might
be leading the legions into battle, it
was he, Caesar, who was the real
leader.

'Wane-ee, weed-ee, week-ee,' he
said, quite a few times after a victory
(for that is how modern scholars
believe the words '*Veni, vidi, vici*' were

pronounced by the ancient Romans
– words which meant '*I* came, *I* saw,
I conquered').

In fact he was reminding his
officers that the credit for the victory
was his, not the goat's.

But behind his back, they, knowing
the reason for the animal's awful
smell, joked that what the goat
would say was, 'Wane-ee, weed-ee,
wee-wee.'

The goat was not only of value on
the field of battle. Caesar found
another use for it. Discipline in the
Roman army was very strict, and
punishments ranged from ten strokes
of the *Felis nonecauda* (which, loosely
translated, means cat-o'-nine-tails) to
as many as a hundred. More serious

misconduct was punishable by death, usually by having your head cut off, though officers committing such crimes were required to fall upon their own swords.

None of these penalties were much fun (certainly not for the guilty party), but one day something took place that cheered things up a bit.

It so happened that one of Caesar's commanders wanted a message taken to the general, and who should volunteer to carry it but that little creep Oleaginus. As before, he found Caesar in his tent, at his side the goat, in the background the Centurion-Capricorn (once a strong and healthy man, but now pale and thin through loss of appetite). Oleaginus delivered the message, bowed low in his smarmy way, and turned to leave the tent.

Something about the rear view of the little legionary sparked off a sudden reaction in the brain of the goat and it charged across the floor of the tent, head down. Its great

curved horns struck Oleaginus squarely on the backside, and he went flying out through the tent-flap.

Once the general and his Centurion-Capricorn and his bodyguard and everyone else near by had stopped laughing, it occurred to Caesar that here was an excellent form of punishment for minor offences, such as improperly shined sandals or poorly polished shields, offences that didn't really merit a beating with the *Felis nonecauda*. It would be much more fun for everyone (except

the victim) to order one butt from
Caesar's goat.

News of this soon spread through

the legions, and from then on it was remarkable to see, at punishment parades, just how many offenders were sent by their centurions to receive this novel come-uppance. For onlookers it was great entertainment, and for Caesar's goat it was a useful form of exercise.

The miscreant was made to stand with his back to the goat, his tunic hitched up to expose his bottom. Then, at the command 'Forward!' (a Celtic word that Caesar had learned during his campaigns in Britain in 55 and 54 BC), the Centurion-Capricorn would release the goat.

Before long, this novel punishment became a recognized sport. Measurements began to be kept of how far the goat could knock a wrongdoer. Bets were laid, and, however badly bruised, it was a proud man who held the current All-Comers' Long Butt record.

Caesar was extremely pleased with his goat and issued another order forbidding anyone else to own such an animal.

'Just as there is only one man called Julius Caesar,' he said to the commanders of his three legions, 'so there will only ever be one goat in Caesar's army.'

'Called what, O great Caesar?' someone said.

'Hm. Yes. Come to think of it,' said Caesar, 'it really ought to have a name. Can anyone suggest a suitable one?'

The commanders hesitated. They all knew the sort of names they'd like to call the goat, such as 'Ponger' or 'Niffy' or 'Stinkbomb'. But none of them wanted to risk being told to fall upon his sword. So they suggested complimentary names like 'Braveheart' and 'Stronghorn' and 'Conqueror'. But Caesar didn't seem to like any of them.

'I can see I'll have to choose a name myself,' he said.

He thought for a while and then

suddenly smacked his forehead and smiled broadly.

'*Habeo solutionem!*' he cried (which, loosely translated, means 'I've got it!').

'What, O great Caesar?' they asked.

'Well, what's yellow and greasy and you spread it on your bread?' he asked.

'Butter,' they replied.

'And what does this goat do?'

Resisting, one and all, the desire to say, 'Stink!' they replied, 'Butt.'

'Well, then,' said Caesar, 'that's it. Its name is Butter.'

The commanders looked at one another.

'Oh,' they said.

Then they looked at Caesar and saw that he thought this was the greatest of jokes.

'Oh, yes!' they all said hastily. 'Oh, ha ha ha! Oh, HA HA HA HA!'

Chapter Four

In the winter of 47 BC, Julius Caesar took a holiday. He needed a rest from constant battles and decided to go to Egypt, for a variety of reasons.

The Egyptians, he had heard, were well disposed towards goats, so he thought Butter would like it. He wanted to see the Pyramids and the

Sphinx, monuments that were far, far older than anything Rome had to offer, and also to see the Nile, the greatest river in the known world.

But mainly (though he didn't let on about this) he wanted to have a look at Cleopatra, Queen of Egypt, who was supposed to be the most beautiful woman of all time.

So Caesar set sail for Alexandria, accompanied by Butter and the Centurion-Capricorn, and the bodyguard, and a couple of cohorts just to be on the safe side.

Little did he know that Cleopatra, like him, had problems relating to the nose. His was large and Roman and a bit bent, hers was small and straight and pretty. He, as we know, had absolutely no sense of smell, she an excellent one.

But it was what she liked to smell, and to smell of, that was the trouble.

Cleopatra, you see, had no use for sweet-smelling ointments and perfumes, and the kind of fragrant scents that women usually like to put upon themselves. She preferred really strong, powerful stinks from which most people would run a mile.

Of all the bad smells in the world, the worst is said to be that of Siberian wolf's urine. Cleopatra had supplies regularly imported to use as her own personal scent.

It was therefore not surprising that there was a great lack of suitors for the (very smelly) hand of this so beautiful Queen.

Cleopatra, receiving news that Julius Caesar was about to arrive, hoped that this eminent Roman soldier might be different from the fine gentlemen of her court, who all smelt so horribly clean.

I do hope he doesn't wash, she said to herself. I long for a man with really fruity body odour. Little did she guess what treats were in store for her.

When Caesar's fleet docked at Alexandria, the first thing he did was to send a message to Queen Cleopatra, announcing his arrival and requesting to meet her. This being granted, Caesar stepped ashore and set out for Cleopatra's palace.

He took his bodyguard with him,
but left the goat behind in the
care of the Centurion-Capricorn.
Who could tell? Butter might take
a dislike to the Egyptian Queen
as he had to Oleaginus. Just
imagine!

Once within the palace, Caesar
was welcomed by the Comptroller of
the Queen's Household, who
somehow managed by a supreme
effort of will to disguise his disgust at
the rank smell surrounding this
distinguished visitor. Caesar, of
course, through constant association
with his goat, smelt just as bad as it
did, if not worse.

'Greetings, O Caesar!' gasped the
Comptroller, mopping his eyes. 'Pray

follow me to Her Majesty's boudoir, for it is her wish that you and she meet alone.' He led the way along a maze of corridors until he stopped at a gilded door, opened it, ushered Caesar in and closed the door again behind the general.

There was thus no witness of that first meeting between Caesar and Cleopatra, but there was equally no doubt of the immediate effect of the one upon the other.

Caesar saw before him a vision of incomparable loveliness, elegantly dressed in rich silks, a jewelled crown upon her dark hair.

He heard the music of her husky voice as she greeted him.

He felt, as he took her hand and

bowed over it to kiss it, the velvety
softness of her skin.

But he knew nothing at all of the
smell of that skin, liberally drenched

41

as it was in Siberian wolf's urine.

By Jupiter! he thought. What a woman!

Cleopatra saw before her the short, stocky figure (for Julius Caesar was but three cubits tall – about five foot, that's to say) of a balding middle-aged man with a broken nose.

Nothing much to look at, she thought, but by Osiris and Isis, he stinks to high heaven! What a whiff, what a pong! It's enough to knock you down! How can I resist such a foul-smelling man?

And so they fell in love, Caesar at first sight, Cleopatra at first sniff.

Chapter Five

When Cleopatra first came to meet
Julius Caesar's goat, the Centurion-
Capricorn had the animal on a
collar and chain, with strict
instructions to hang on tight. Caesar
didn't want to risk any unfortunate
incident.

In fact, however, Butter was well

behaved on first introduction to the Queen. He merely stood with raised head, his rubbery lips curled back, his yellow eyes half closed, and sniffed appreciatively at the strange strong scent of the lady.

As for Cleopatra, she was delighted. By the great King Cheops! she said to herself. This Julius Caesar even has his own matching accessory, a designer goat that smells exactly as he does! What a man!

'Do you like him, Clee?' asked Caesar (already they had pet names for each other).

'Oh yes, Jujube!' cried Cleopatra. 'I just love the way he smells!'

'And how does he smell, would

you say?' asked Caesar.

'Like you.'

'And how do I smell, would you say?'

'Gorgeous!' said the Queen of Egypt. 'Almost as gorgeous as me. You do like the way I smell, don't you, Jujube?'

Caesar sniffed deeply. Can't smell a damned thing, he thought, but I mustn't let on.

'Wonderful, Clee,' he said. 'Wonderful.'

At the end of his Egyptian holiday, Caesar set sail for Italy, accompanied by his goat, the Centurion-Capricorn, the bodyguard, the two cohorts and, you won't be surprised to hear, Cleopatra.

So now it was the wretched people of Rome who had to put up with the awful combined stinks of Caesar, his goat and his lady-love.

One look (from a distance) at Cleopatra and the Romans said to one another, 'She's beautiful!'

One sniff at her (close up) and they couldn't wait to be out of range for a breath of fresh air and to say to one another, 'By Jupiter! What a pong! How can Caesar stand that?'

'How can she stand the smell of him, for that matter?'

'To say nothing of that goat!'

'She's the worst, by a league!'

'She never washes, they say!'

'Never?'

'No, and never takes a bath!'

This last, the Romans found out a little later, was not strictly true. Cleopatra did indeed not wash. She considered that her imported Siberian scent was much too costly to be regularly rinsed away. But once a month, at the full moon, she took a bath.

She had not been in Rome many days before she said to Caesar, 'By the way, Jujube, in a couple of weeks' time the moon will be full and I shall be having my bath. Get it all fixed up for me, will you?'

'No problem, Clee,' said Caesar. 'I have a fine bathhouse in my mansion. The pool in it holds a hundred gallons of water. I'll have it heated to whatever temperature you wish. They won't need two weeks' notice.'

'They will,' said Cleopatra. 'The Queen of Egypt does not bathe in water.'

'Oh,' said Caesar. 'Well, what do you bathe in?'

'Milk.'

'Cow's milk?'

'No, ass's milk.'

'Oh,' said Caesar. 'I see,' he said (though he didn't). 'Still that won't take two weeks. I'll issue an order straightaway, ordering every she-ass in Rome and district that is presently suckling a foal to be rounded up and milked. We should be able to get a hundred gallons of fresh ass's milk in a couple of days.'

'Oh, Jujube!' said Cleopatra.
'Don't be such a donkey! I don't
want fresh ass's milk. It's got to have
time to go sour, to go off, to curdle,
to get really fruity. That's the way I
like it.'

'Oh,' said Caesar. 'I see,' he said
(though he didn't). Perhaps that way
it's good for her skin, he thought.

He could not know what
Cleopatra had long ago discovered.
Though her imported Siberian scent
might be supposed – by other people
– to be the worst smell in the world,
it could be made even more awful –
more lovely to her – if it was applied
over a coating of really sour ass's
milk.

Thus, when she emerged from her monthly bath, she would not allow her handmaidens to dry her. Instead they must immediately spray her milk-soaked skin with Siberian wolf's urine.

The order which Caesar now issued required all those who could supply ass's milk to bring their donkeys to the Colosseum. The Romans loved a good spectacle (usually of people killing one another or being killed by wild beasts like lions), but Caesar thought that an ass-milking competition might be a nice change and rather fun, and could attract a good crowd.

Accordingly, he offered two prizes of money. The *denarius* was the chief

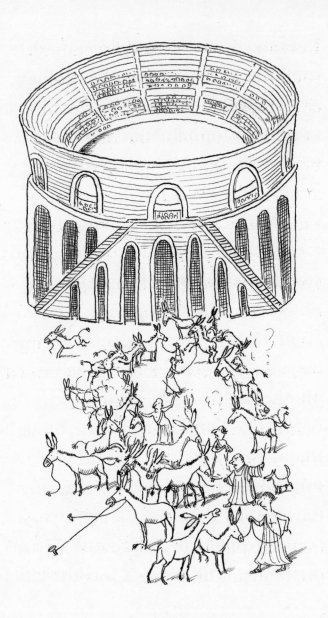

Roman silver coin (oddly enough, each was worth ten smaller coins called *asses*), and Caesar offered a hundred *denarii* for the man who milked his donkey quickest, and another hundred for the owner of the donkey that gave the most milk.

On the day, not surprisingly, the donkey mares were upset at being taken to a strange place, to be milked by hand instead of suckling their foals, in front of a great crowd of cheering onlookers. Being donkeys, they behaved as stubbornly and as awkwardly as possible, kicking the milk pails over, kicking the

milkers and biting
them, and
escaping from
their handlers
to gallop
round the Colosseum, kicking and
biting other donkeys as they went.

But the crowd loved it, and the
prizes were awarded, and at last a
hundred gallons of ass's milk were
collected and taken to Caesar's
mansion where the milk was poured
into the square stone pool in his
bath-house.

The weather in Rome was very
hot that summer, and the milk began
to go off very quickly. By the time of
the full moon, the pong in Caesar's
bathhouse was unbearable to

everyone (except Caesar, who couldn't smell it, and Cleopatra, who thought it heavenly).

The Centurion-Capricorn – who, after all, had to put up with more day-to-day stink than anyone else – summed up the general feeling. '*Dum spiro, spero*,' he said (which, loosely translated, means 'As long as I'm still breathing, there's hope').

There was, however, something else happening during those two weeks while the asses' milk was going bad. Butter was beginning to suffer from two of the seven deadly sins.

The first was envy. To begin with, Julius Caesar's goat had not thought much about this new woman that had come into his master's life. But day by day he became increasingly jealous of the Queen of Egypt.

Time was when Caesar spent all his spare moments with his goat. Now he spent them all with Cleopatra. Butter did not like this state of affairs at all. Which led him to the second deadly sin – anger.

By the time that the moon was full, on the day in fact when Cleopatra was to take her bath, Butter's feelings towards her were as hostile as they could possibly be.

In the bathhouse, the scene was set.

Cleopatra stood at the edge of the pool full of foul-smelling, curdled ass's milk. Around her were gathered her handmaidens, waiting to remove her robes and then to assist her as she walked down the steps into the pool.

The only other person in the bathhouse was Julius Caesar, who thought it would be fun to stand behind a pillar and play Peeping Tom.

Just at that moment, Butter came in, trailing a length of rope. The Centurion-Capricorn had tied him up (on Caesar's orders), but the goat had chewed through the tether.

Now, at the precise moment when the handmaidens had removed the Queen's robes and she had taken her first step into the pool, Julius Caesar's goat set eyes on the rear

view of his master's new favourite.

Such was the force with which
Butter's horns struck the royal
bottom that Cleopatra was
catapulted far out into the deep end,
and disappeared under the horrid
mess of clotted curds and watery

whey, to surface again, spluttering
and gasping. The handmaidens ran
wildly about, in their hands the royal
clothing, while one of them carried
a great glass phial filled ready with
Siberian wolf's urine.

Then to the ears of the furious

Queen there came, from behind a pillar, the sound of someone giggling, and the giggle became a chuckle, and the chuckle became a gale of laughter as Julius Caesar stepped forth, rocking about in hysterical mirth at the sight before his streaming eyes.

'Oh, Clee!' he gasped. 'You've easily beaten the All-Comers' Long Butt record!'

So long and loudly did he roar that all the members of his household, and even passers-by from the street, came running to see what the joke was. They too all burst into loud guffaws at the sight of the smelly Queen floundering furiously about in a sea of stinking ass's milk.

Caesar should have known better. No one likes to be laughed at in public, and no one likes it less than a queen.

Cleopatra caught the next boat back to Alexandria.

Chapter Six

Everyone (except the general) was heartily glad to see the back of the Queen of Egypt. Butter had been particularly pleased to see the back of her.

Had she stayed, who can tell how different the future might have been for Julius Caesar? But as it was, he

too now began to suffer from another
of the seven deadly sins – pride.

For some time he had been
admired by the people and by the
soldiery, as victorious generals
commonly are. Winning every battle
is a sure way to popularity, even if
you smell as bad as, thanks to his
goat, Caesar did. Again thanks to
the goat, all these battles were won
with hardly any casualties amongst
Caesar's legionaries, for the enemy
always ran away from the terrible
smell borne towards them on the
wind.

No wonder then that the general
became increasingly pleased with
himself, and during the years 46 and
45 BC (when he easily defeated the

remnants of Pompey's armies), he declared himself the dictator of the Roman Empire.

Supreme power was his, riches were his, everyone scurried to do his slightest bidding. The world, it seemed, was his oyster.

Like many dictators, however, he was lonely. Everyone kowtowed to him, but nobody really liked him. Except his goat.

He had no one to talk to, again except his goat, so he took to having long chats to it.

'Wouldn't Mater and Pater be amazed if they could see me now, Butter?' he would say. 'Look at it this way. The Roman Empire is the most powerful force in the whole world. I am the most powerful man in the Roman Empire. *Ergo*, I am the most powerful man in the world! *Quod erat demonstrandum!*' (which, loosely translated, means 'Therefore, that proves it!').

On the minus side, Caesar, like all dictators, had his enemies.

In the senate, the governing body of ancient Rome, there were a number of men who viewed Julius Caesar's puffed-up pride with dismay. These senators suspected that Caesar, not content with being dictator, had his eye on an even higher position: to become, in fact, the monarch of all he surveyed, to be Emperor.

Of these senators, two in

particular were one hundred *per centum* anti-Caesar.

One of them was none other than that very Brutus who had, more than forty years ago, clobbered Caesar's sense of smell with that overhead kick.

The other, Cassius by name, had also been at North Rome Primary School at the same time. He had a reputation for twisting smaller boys' arms or stamping on their toes.

Now they made a fine pair, united by their jealousy of Caesar and their desire to take him down a peg.

'He's become a proper bighead,' said Brutus.

'Too big for his boots as well,' said Cassius.

'He must be removed.'

'Removed? You mean ...'

'No, no,' said Brutus. 'Not what you're thinking, Cassius. For that we would pay with our lives. No, there must be some way to limit his powers.'

'I wish we could limit the smell of the fellow,' said Cassius. 'Him and his goat.'

But in fact it was Julius Caesar's goat who, all unknowingly, decided the fate of his master.

It happened like this.

One fine day Caesar was out for a walk with Butter. He had given the Centurion-Capricorn the day off, for the goat walked to heel like a well-trained dog, and so they were alone

(or so it appeared, though of course
members of Caesar's bodyguard
were discreetly walking nearby,
trying to look like ordinary citizens
and at the same time trying to keep
upwind of the goat).

As the dictator and his pet walked
by the banks of the River Tiber, who
should they come upon, by chance,
but Brutus and Cassius, sitting on a
bench (just feeding the ducks, it
seemed, though actually they were

busy trying to plot the dictator's downfall).

They looked up, saw Caesar and got to their feet.

'*Salve!*' they cried (which, loosely translated, means 'Hi, there!').

Caesar frowned. He had never liked those two, neither Brutus, for obvious reasons connected with his nose, nor Cassius, who had twisted

69

his arms and stood on his toes.

'We're not in the playground at North Rome Primary now,' he said in his most arrogant voice. 'You will kindly address me in the proper manner.'

Brutus and Cassius, half a cubit taller than the dictator, looked down at him. They looked round, and saw the bodyguard closing quietly in. They looked at one another, and then they forced themselves to offer the proper greeting.

'*Salve*, O great Caesar!' they said.

'That's better,' said Caesar. 'What are you doing here anyway?'

'Just feeding the ducks,' they said, and they turned to face the river, pointing to the quacking birds.

Butter regarded their senatorial backsides. He could tell that his master did not like these men, so, loyally, neither did he. He put his head down and took a run at Brutus and knocked him over the bank and down into the Tiber. Then he did the same to Cassius.

As had happened in the case of Cleopatra and her bath, Caesar thought this one heck of a joke. So, I'm sorry to say, did his bodyguard, who all came running to laugh their heads off at the sight of the two senators sploshing about in the murky water.

With great difficulty, because of their waterlogged togas, Brutus and Cassius somehow struggled to the

bank – the far bank, as far away as they could get from the guffawing spectators.

As they crawled out, covered in various bits of muck, Brutus said once more to Cassius, 'He must be removed.'

In return, Cassius, as before, said, 'Removed? You mean …'

'Yes,' said Brutus. 'This time I do mean exactly what you're thinking,'

and then, as one man, they turned
their thumbs down.

Chapter Seven

There was only one place to do the deed, they decided later, and that was in the senate-house, for the simple reason that only senators were allowed to enter it. Thus, Caesar's bodyguard would not be able to protect him.

Brutus and Cassius called a secret

meeting of a number of hard-faced senators – Casca, Metellus and Cinna among them – who had long wanted to bring down Caesar, and could now be persuaded to help in getting rid of him for ever.

By a strange chance, they settled upon the Ides of March 44 BC – the forty-sixth anniversary of the playground incident – as the day for the deed.

When, that morning, Caesar walked into the senate-house, leaving his bodyguard outside, the conspirators thronged around him with many cries of '*Salve*, O great Caesar!' They were all wearing broad smiles as though delighted to see him, and they pressed closer and closer to the dictator. Then they all drew their swords and plunged them into Caesar's body.

One face amongst those of the assassins swam before the victim's failing sight, and once more he cried, '*Et tu, Brute!*'

Then he uttered his last words, '*Caesar moriturus est!*' (which, precisely translated, means 'Caesar is about to die!') and he did.

Meanwhile, back at Caesar's mansion, Butter, by that strange sixth sense that some animals have, had become worried about his master. Some instinct told him that all was not well, and once more he chewed through his tether, and set off through the streets of Rome, following the trail until he came to the senate-house.

By the time the goat reached the scene of the murder, all the conspirators had fled except Brutus and Cassius. They still stood facing one another on either side of Caesar's body, holding their bloodstained swords and looking down with evil satisfaction at the corpse.

This was what Butter saw as he bounded into the senate-house.

There, directly before him, was one of those senatorial bottoms with which he had dealt so effectively on the banks of the Tiber. He hit it at full speed (it was Brutus's) and the impact hurled the man forward into

Cassius. Both the murderers fell
dead across the body of their victim.

Afterwards, it was the general
opinion that Brutus and Cassius,
appalled at the deed they had done,
had decided, like true Roman
gentlemen, to fall upon their swords.

78

In fact, they had fallen upon each other's.

As for Butter, he bent his great horned head above the body of his master and uttered one low groan of farewell. Then he turned and left the senate-house.

Chapter Eight

If you like happy endings, then I'm afraid the story of Julius Caesar did not have one.

But on the other hand, the story of Julius Caesar's goat did. Once the fuss over the dictator's murder had died down and he had been buried with full military honours, and the rest of the conspirators had dutifully fallen upon their own swords, the senate met to discuss how they could best remember the life of the late, great general.

One of the senators suggested that they should give honours to his beloved pet.

'Caesar would have liked that,' he said. 'Thumbs up, everyone who approves the idea,' and everyone did.

At first they considered making Butter a senator, until they realized that the goat would then have access to the senate-house, stink and all.

Then they decided to make Julius Caesar's goat a proconsul (this was a kind of Roman magistrate with authority outside the city).

'Proconsul of what?' someone asked.

'Of the seven hills,' someone else suggested, for Rome was and still is surrounded by seven hills.

It may not be so nowadays, but in 44 BC great flocks of wild goats roamed these hills. Butter, the senators said to one another, would have a high old time.

And so he did. Being bigger and stronger and a better butter than all the other billy goats, he beat them up and pinched their wives and became the father of umpteen children.

Nor was he the only one to benefit from his newfound freedom, for now

there was no
further
need for
the services of
his minder, the
Centurion-
Capricorn. He
reverted to plain
centurion and lost his
extra one *denarius per diem*, but a fat
lot he cared. At last he was free of
that ghastly pong that, over the last
five years, had destroyed his appetite
and marred his enjoyment of life.
The colour came back into his pale
cheeks and he began to put on
weight.

Butter the proconsul roamed the
Seven Hills of Rome in perfect

freedom and contentment, until he died peacefully in his sleep in 36 BC. He was then fifteen years old (a ripe old age for a ripe old goat). The senators held a meeting to decide what should be done with his body.

'Shall we cremate him?' said somebody. 'Build a huge funeral pyre and stick him on it and set fire to it?'

'Or shall we bury him,' said someone else, 'with the honour due to a proconsul of course, and a fine headstone above his grave?'

'No,' said another senator. 'Tell you what. Let's stuff him.'

So they engaged the services of the leading taxidermist of the day, who made a superb job of it, and they placed the finished article in the

Temple of Jupiter, on the Capitoline Hill.

The great stuffed goat became one of the best-loved sights of the Eternal City, and maters and paters took their kids to see him, himself the father of countless kids.

There he stood in the Capitol, his fine bearded head raised, his great horns thrown back so as almost to touch the (smell-free) ginger hair of his back, his yellow (glass) eyes surveying the city below.

Each year, on the Ides of March, a teacher would bring a class from North Rome Primary up to the Capitol and, pointing at the proud figure of Butter, Proconsul of the Seven Hills, would say, 'Now,

children, who is this?'
    Then loudly, all the children cried:
'IT'S JULIUS CAESAR'S GOAT!!'

Dick King-Smith

Born: Bitton, Gloucestershire
27 March 1922
Jobs: Soldier, farmer, salesman, teacher,
TV presenter and author

When did you start writing?
Started my first book for children, *The Fox Busters*, in 1976, got it published in 1978. Since then I have written so many books that I think I have rather lost count!

Where do you get the ideas for your stories?
Things I've done, people I've met or known, animals I've owned or know, but mostly it's just a question of sitting and thinking.

What are your hobbies?
Writing books for my children. Sitting in the garden on summer evenings with a nice drink. Talking to my dogs. Washing up. You'll never catch me buying a dishwasher; it would take all the fun out of it!

Will you give your three top tips on becoming an author?
- Read as widely as you can. Try not to read rubbish, but soak up all sorts of good stories.
- Practise. No good saying, 'I'm going to be a writer'. Get on with it. Write about whatever you fancy.
- Show what you've done to someone whose opinion you respect – Mum, Dad, your teacher. Listen to their comments: don't get upset by them, think about them.

And finally, if you hadn't been a writer, what do you think you would have been?
A farmer still. I'm glad I'm not now, I'm too blooming old to be humping sacks of corn or pitching bales; and I shouldn't like to go back to milking cows. I wish I still had some pigs though...

Read more in Puffin

For complete information about books available from Puffin – and Penguin – and how to order them, contact us at the appropriate address below. Please note that for copyright reasons the selection of books varies from country to country.

www.puffin.co.uk

In the United Kingdom: Please write to Dept EP, Penguin Books Ltd, Bath Road, Harmondsworth, West Drayton, Middlesex UB7 ODA

In the United States: Please write to Penguin Group (USA), Inc., P.O. Box 12289, Dept B, Newark, New Jersey 07101–5289 or call 1–800–788–6262

In Canada: Please write to Penguin Books Canada Ltd, 10 Alcorn Avenue, Suite 300, Toronto, Ontario M4V 3B2

In Australia: Please write to Penguin Books Australia Ltd, 250 Camberwell Road, Camberwell, Victoria 3124

In New Zealand: Please write to Penguin Books (NZ) Ltd, Private Bag 102902, North Shore Mail Centre, Auckland 10

In India: Please write to Penguin Books India Pvt Ltd, 11 Panscheel Shopping Centre, Panscheel Park, New Delhi 110 017

In the Netherlands: Please write to Penguin Books Netherlands bv, Postbus 3507, NL–1001 AH Amsterdam

In Germany: Please write to Penguin Books Deutschland GmbH, Metzlerstrasse 26, 60594 Frankfurt am Main

In Spain: Please write to Penguin Books S. A., Bravo Murillo 19, 1° B, 28015 Madrid

In Italy: Please write to Penguin Italia s.r.l., Via Felice Casati 20, I–20124 Milano

In France: Please write to Penguin France S. A., 17 rue Lejeune, F–31000 Toulouse

In Japan: Please write to Penguin Books Japan, Ishikiribashi Building, 2–5–4, Suido, Bunkyo-ku, Tokyo 112

In South Africa: Please write to Longman Penguin Southern Africa (Pty) Ltd, Private Bag X08, Bertsham 2013